Shadow Over Mousehaven Manor

by Mary DeBall Kwitz

illustrated by Stella Ormai

AN
APPLE
PAPERBACK

SCHOLASTIC INC.

New York   Toronto   London   Auckland   Sydney

ISBN 0-590-42033-X

12 11 10 9 8 7 6 5 4 3   3 4 5/9

Printed in the U.S.A.   40

Contents

Beware of vampire bats, creeping cats, and Chicago rats.

1.
A Chill
Winter's Night

Minabell Mouse opened her front door and peered out into the night. "Aunt Pitty Pat?" she called softly.

The only answer was the sound of the prairie wind blowing down Mole Hill Lane. The wind shook the branches of the oak tree overhead and sent powdered snow drifting down in front of her cottage.

Minabell stepped out on her porch and looked down the lane. Smoke curled above cottage rooftops, and light glowed from windows hung with holiday decorations. But no creature was on the road. She shivered and hurried inside.

She had been mistaken. No one had knocked on the door. It had been the wind shaking the latch. But where was Aunt Pitty Pat? She should have arrived today from Mousedale. Minabell checked the calendar on the wall. It was the twenty-second of December, the day her aunt always came to spend the holidays with her. This time it would be a very special occasion. Aunt Pitty Pat was bringing her new husband, Magnus, to visit.

Minabell glanced about her cottage. Everything was ready. The Christmas tree was decorated and brightly lit, and her presents were gift wrapped and placed beneath the tree. All that was needed to complete the picture was Aunt Pitty Pat and Uncle Magnus sitting before the fire, sipping cups of hot, sweet clover tea.

Which reminded Minabell — it was time for supper. She put the kettle on to boil and spread strawberry jam on a piece of toast. She had just started singing one of her favorite songs, "Christmas Bells Ring O'er the Prairie," when she heard footsteps on the porch. A moment later there came a loud knocking. "Aunt Pitty Pat!" she cried, running to open the door.

Minabell let out a small sigh of disappointment. There on her doorstep was Rodentville's mailbird, Gaylord Cardinal. Head down against the wind, he stood shaking in the cold with a letter in his claw.

"Neither snow, nor rain, nor gloom of night stays the mailbird in his appointed flights," he muttered.

Suddenly realizing that Minabell had opened the door, he snapped to attention. "Special delivery for Ms. Minabell Mouse," he said in his most official voice.

"For me? Imagine that!" exclaimed Minabell. She dearly loved getting mail, but had never received a special delivery letter in her whole life. She twitched her whiskers excitedly and peered at the envelope, wondering who had sent it. The light in the doorway was too dim to make out the handwriting.

Gaylord couldn't contain his curiosity. "Aren't you going to open it?" he asked, flapping his wings to keep warm.

"Come in out of the cold, Gaylord," said Minabell. "I was just about to make a cup of tea. Won't you join me?" she asked warmly, putting the letter in her apron pocket. She didn't want to share it with anyone.

Gaylord raised his headcrest and glared at Minabell. A sudden flurry of snow made him glance up at the threatening sky. "I think I'd better be getting home while I can still fly in this wind," he said.

The storm was getting worse. Minabell struggled to close the door against the strong draft. But before she did, she called out a cheery, "Merry Christmas to you and your wife, Gaylord."

"A joyous Noël from the Cardinal family," replied Gaylord as he lifted off. And the sound of his voice was carried back to Minabell on the wind.

Humming happily to herself, Minabell opened her cupboard and took down a cup and a jar of sweet clover tea. She put a teaspoon of tea in the cup and filled it with bubbling hot water from the kettle. She put the cup and a piece of toast on a plate, carried it to the parlor table, and drew up her rocking chair.

She sat down, placing the special delivery letter next to her plate. Then she had a sip of hot tea and read the outside of the envelope.

From:
Mr. Magnus Mouse
Mousehaven Manor
Mousedale, Illinois 62704

SPECIAL   To:
DELIVERY   Ms. Minabell Mouse
           136 Mole Hole Drive
           Rodentville, Illinois 60148

13

The letter was from Uncle Magnus, her new uncle. With an anxious frown, Minabell slit open the envelope.

Mousedale, Illinois
December 21

Dear Minabell,

Although we have never met, I take pen in paw to send you warmest holiday greetings.

But unfortunately, my dear niece, I have very sad news. Your poor Aunt Pitty Pat has been gravely ill. And now she has taken a turn for the worse.

Her last wish is that she might see you, her only remaining relative, to say good-bye.

She tells me that she left her will with you. She asks that you bring it with you when you come.

Hurry, I fear the end is near.

Your most devoted,

Uncle Magnus

P.S. Do not forget the will.

Minabell vaguely heard the wind whipping about the cottage eaves and whistling down the chimney. But all was quiet in the little parlor. There was only the tick of the clock on the mantle and the occasional crackle of logs on the fire.

She gazed at the framed wedding picture of Aunt Pitty Pat and Uncle Magnus standing on the table next to her cup. Judging by the photograph, Uncle Magnus was the largest mouse she had ever seen. A huge, shaggy-furred rodent, he towered over her aunt, making her appear even smaller than she actually was.

Dear, plump little Aunt Pitty Pat, the kindest and most loving aunt a mouse could ever have. And now she was very ill, perhaps dying. A tear ran down Minabell's face and through her silken side-whiskers.

Just at that moment the storm burst over the prairie in full force. Overhead the ancient oak tree bent to the gale. And with a roar and a grinding crash, Minabell's parlor roof caved in. The Christmas tree lights went out, and cup, toast, furniture, and presents scattered in all directions.

With a terrified squeal, Minabell fell over backward in her rocker. Still clutching the letter, she darted into the bedroom. There was another crash, and part of the bedroom ceiling collapsed, crushing the bed and sealing off the door.

The overturned clock in the parlor ticked on, and the wind and the snow blew down through the hole in the roof.

2.
Trapped

Minabell sat up slowly in the dark. She lifted a shaking paw and touched the bump on the back of her head. "Ohhh!" she moaned softly. She stared blindly into the darkness and waited for the pain to subside.

Struggling to her feet, she groped her way forward and bumped into her chest of drawers. Holding onto its edge, she inched around the chest to where the bedroom door should have been. It was now covered with a jumble of earth, stones, and timber. Then she heard the faint sounds of digging and familiar voices. With a cry of relief, Minabell threw herself on the pile of rubble and began pushing it aside.

"Quiet!" said a voice on the other side. "I think I hear something." There was a pause, and then someone cleared his throat. "Minabell, this is your mailbird speaking. Are you in there?"

"I'm here! I'm here!" shouted Minabell, shoving a boulder out of the way.

"She's alive!" cried Mrs. Olivia Cardinal, Gaylord's wife.

"Hold on, Minabell. We're digging you out," called out Teena Chipmunk, Minabell's very best friend in the whole village.

"Back off," growled the familiar voice of Mumbles Mole, her landlord. "Let a body in here who knows how to dig."

Minabell heard the steady, comforting sound of Mumbles shoveling the earth away with his paws. In a few minutes he had burrowed a hole big enough for her to scramble out and right into the arms of Teena Chipmunk.

In the dim light of a lantern, held high by Mrs. Cardinal, Minabell looked around at the worried faces of her friends.

"Are you all right, Minabell?" Teena Chipmunk held her friend at arm's length and peered anxiously into her face. "Nothing broken?"

"I'm fine," said Minabell rather shakily. She decided not to mention the bump she had received on the back of her head. The throbbing had stopped, and the injury did not appear to be serious. No need to cause unnecessary alarm.

She glanced about at her parlor and caught her breath in dismay. "Look at my house!" she cried. "What happened?"

"A branch from the oak tree broke loose in the blizzard," Teena said. "It fell on your roof."

"Squashed it flat," said Mumbles.

"It was dreadful," said Mrs. Cardinal. "The crash shook the whole village. But your house was the only one hit. We thought you were done for, Minabell."

Gaylord Cardinal puffed out his breast-feathers and paced back and forth. "As a duly elected official of Rodentville, I wish to inform you, Ms. Mouse, that the village is not responsible for . . ."

"Baloney," growled Mumbles.

"Is not responsible, I say," continued Gaylord, with a withering glance in Mumbles' direction, "for any damages brought about by the storm." He raised his headcrest and fanned it out for maximum effect.

"My dear," Mrs. Cardinal twittered, "remember your high blood pressure."

"Not only as your mailbird," continued Gaylord, ignoring his wife's remark, "but as the state bird of Illinois, I officially wash my claws of the whole affair."

Mumbles squinted nearsightedly at Gaylord and snorted. "While your mailbird is washin' his claws, your landlord is gonna rebuild from the ground up. Come spring, Minabell, you'll have the strongest house in the village, or my name ain't Mumbles Mudhouse Mole."

Gaylord lowered his crest and his voice. "Off the record, Minabell, Mrs. Cardinal and I want to offer our heartfelt sympathy. If there is anything we can do to help, unofficially speaking of course, please let us know."

Minabell looked up at the gaping hole in the ceiling and wasn't comforted. Although the storm had run its course, snow was still falling. It drifted silently down through the dark hole, covering the broken furniture with a blanket of white.

"Oh, dear!" Minabell cried. "What shall I do?"

Teena put an arm around her. "You must come and live with me until your house is repaired," she said firmly. "That's what friends are for. It will be fun having someone to share Christmas with."

"Christmas!" Minabell ran to the spot where she had left her beautifully wrapped gifts. She found them buried beneath the tree limb, crushed beyond recovery.

"Never mind, Minabell," Mrs. Cardinal said. "We'll have a Christmas party, and you'll be the guest of honor. Everybody knows the guest of honor doesn't bring gifts, she receives them."

"That's right," Gaylord said, and Mumbles nodded in agreement.

A full moon rode over the hole above and shone down on the little group of friends. Suddenly Minabell remembered the special delivery letter from her Uncle Magnus.

With Teena lighting the way, she scrambled back over the rubble into her bedroom. She found the tearstained letter and the wedding picture where they had fallen next to her crushed bed.

Much to Gaylord's satisfaction, Minabell

read the letter out loud. "I must leave for Mousehaven Manor tomorrow," she added worriedly. She breathed a silent prayer to herself: I hope I arrive in time.

The hour was late, and everyone was tired and chilled. With good nights and wide yawns all around, they went off to bed.

Teena took Minabell's little paw in hers and led her from the wreckage. They walked in silence through the moonlight to Teena's cottage and woodworking shop on the edge of town. Teena gently tucked Minabell into her own warm sparrow-down bed and banked the fire in the hearth. Soon the two friends fell into an exhausted sleep.

Early the next morning Minabell went back to the ruins to gather supplies for her coming trip. Luckily the chest of drawers was still intact. She was able to find several pairs of clean white mittens and her brush, comb, and toothbrush. She also took her most prized possession, her state flag of Illinois. She found it in the bottom drawer, neatly folded and ready for packing. With these items, and her sleeping bag, she felt ready for the journey ahead.

Suddenly, amidst all the hurried preparations, she remembered. Aunt Pitty Pat's will!

3.
Leaving Home

Minabell looked everywhere for the will. Climbing over the fallen oak branch, she searched through closets and cupboards. She pulled the drawers from the chest and dumped the contents on the floor.

But the will had disappeared. Or rather, she thought worriedly, the spot where I had so carefully hidden it for safekeeping has vanished from my memory.

She sat down on the branch to think. She tried to remember back to the day, so long ago, when Aunt Pitty Pat had given her the will and told her to guard it with her life.

"It's your inheritance, Minabell," she had said. "It's more precious than a gold prairie pebble or your state flag. Never let it out of your paws." How solemn her aunt had looked when she had handed her the will.

"Then what happened?" wondered Minabell out loud. "Of course!" She remembered now. She had done what Illinois mice have always done when they have wanted to remember a secret hiding place forever and ever. She had recited the Remembering Rhyme and performed the Magic Brow-Writing Trick.

She remembered closing her eyes, turning around three times, and reciting:

"Three times I twirl
For rodent luck.
Three times I twirl
With rodent pluck.
I'll never reveal
This secret space.
I'll never forget
This hiding place."

With her eyes still shut, she had written with an imaginary pencil the letters *C-E-L-L-A-R* on her forehead. Then she had climbed down to her root cellar and placed her aunt's will next to a storage bin.

Minabell laughed. "Holy prairie fire! I'm practically sitting on the will."

She quickly scraped away the snow in front of the hearth and pushed back the wet rug. And there it was, the trapdoor to her root cellar. She lifted the door and climbed down the ladder.

Light coming from above dimly lit the small room. Fragrant bundles of dried herbs hung from the ceiling beams. Row upon row of bins lined the walls. They were filled with acorns, crab apples, wild onions, and dandelion roots. The rolled-up will was wedged into a crevice between two of the bins, just as she had left it.

She stood in the half light recalling Aunt Pitty Pat and happier times.

She remembered how her aunt had urged her to visit Mousehaven Manor, the home of her ancestors. But she had never had the courage to leave her friends and travel so far. Minabell, in fact, had never traveled more than a few mousemiles from Rodentville.

She sighed. She was finally going to make the trip to Mousedale. But perhaps now it would be too late. "I pray I'll arrive in time, Aunt Pitty Pat," she whispered. Minabell squared her shoulders and picked up the will. Then she hurried up the ladder and out into the sunlight of Mole Hill Lane.

As a crimson sun set behind the oak tree, Minabell stood at the edge of the village saying good-bye to her friends.

Gaylord placed a wingtip on her paw. "I don't want to alarm you, Minabell, but during my postal flights I've noticed strange comings and goings across the state. There seems to be more traffic than usual moving south toward Mousedale. It might be wise to travel only on Rodent Run." He looked at her with concern, leaned over, and whispered in her ear, "Don't speak to strangers, and be on the lookout for Chicago rats."

Suddenly remembering his official duties, Gaylord tipped his mailbird's cap. "Ms. Mouse, on behalf of the village of Rodentville, I bid you a fond farewell. May you have a pleasant journey and a safe return."

Mrs. Cardinal made comforting little chirping noises as she gathered Minabell in a feathery embrace.

"Give our love to your Aunt Pitty Pat," she murmured, handing Minabell a bag of acornburgers. "Some food for your trip, my dear." She gave her an extra little squeeze and added, "Now be careful crossing Interstate 55."

Mumbles shuffled forward. "So long, Minabell. Keep your eyes peeled for city slickers."

Minabell gave him a hug.

"Aw, shucks," he said.

Minabell looked around. "Where is Teena Chipmunk?"

"Wait! Wait! I'm coming." Teena came running down Mole Hill Lane carrying a big package. She skidded to a stop in front of Minabell. "Sorry I'm late," she gasped. "I was wrapping your Christmas present." She thrust it into Minabell's paws.

It was a long, narrow package taller than Minabell. "It's not to be opened until Christmas," Teena said. "I hope you'll like it."

Minabell laughed. "Christmas!" she protested. "But that means I'll have to carry this huge thing for two nights and a day."

Teena was firm. Christmas presents were meant to be opened on Christmas morning and not before. After some struggling, she managed to push the package lengthwise through the straps of Minabell's backpack.

Teena gave the package a final pat into place. "Merry Christmas, Minabell. Have a *speedy* journey," she added with a funny little wink.

As the moon came from behind a cloud, paws were seen furtively brushing away tears.

With a heavy heart, Minabell ducked under a split rail fence and started on her journey.

Walking across the field, she heard the strains of the Illinois state song. Looking back, she saw Gaylord leading everyone in a song of farewell.

"By thy rivers gently flowing,
Illinois, Illinois
O'er thy prairies verdant growing
Illinois, Illinois
Comes an echo on the breeze,
Rustling through the leafy trees
And its mellow tones were these,
Illinois, Illinois."

This was the last sound Minabell heard as she left the prairie and entered Rodent Run.

4.
Moonlight Meeting

Rodent Run had been built in pioneer days by the great Geronimouse, ancestor of all Illinois mice. The narrow, covered passageway, made of tightly woven prairie grass, was always kept in good repair. It ran alongside Interstate 55 from Chicago in the north, southward to Springfield, the state capital.

The Run was just the right size for mice, moles, and chipmunks. But it was too small for large creatures such as cats, dogs, and, Minabell hoped, Chicago rats. The passageway was so well hidden, by weeds in the summer and snow in the winter, that small creatures considered it the safest way to travel even though it might take them a bit out of their way.

Minabell, who had never traveled very far on Rodent Run, stepped through the entrance and looked about anxiously. Moonlight filtering down through the arched ceiling dimly lit the long corridor before her. There were no other travelers in sight. Heartened, she took a final look at her state map, adjusted her backpack, and started on her journey.

She walked at a brisk pace and by midnight had traveled many mousemiles. The few creatures she met were going in the opposite direction. Minabell decided they probably were on their way to Chicago to spend the Christmas holidays with friends and relatives. She remembered Gaylord's advice and didn't speak to anyone. But she couldn't resist a shy nod now and then.

For their part, they were a closemouthed bunch. Arms full of packages, they hurried along with downcast eyes. The friendly country creatures were unnaturally silent as if they, too, had been cautioned not to speak to strangers.

Minabell took Gaylord's other piece of advice more seriously. "Be on the lookout for Chicago rats," he had warned. She had never met a Chicago rat and was anxious to keep it that way. She had heard they were large, ugly rodents and hardened criminals. It was said they overran every alley and basement of the great city. It was even whispered that they had invaded the very heart of Chicago, City Hall itself.

Minabell shuddered. This was only gossip, of course. Some of her best friends were rats. She thought fondly of several wood rats she knew living in Rodentville. Harmless, peace-loving citizens they were, too. Gaylord worried too much, she decided.

The corridor stretched out of sight before her, an endless, weary way. There should have been plenty of space to pass other travelers, with room to spare. But Teena's Christmas gift, sticking out on either side of her backpack, made this impossible. Minabell had to flatten herself against the wall to allow her fellow travelers to get by.

At first she didn't mind. But after several hours of stepping aside, she grew tired and longed to be rid of the gift. What was in this long, thin package? Minabell wondered. What could be so important that she must carry it with her? Teena was her dearest friend, but she could be very impractical.

Occupied with her thoughts, Minabell walked all night and through the long hours of the next day. She didn't stop, not even to eat, until the sun had set, and the moon was again lighting the corridor.

Finally she realized that she was too exhausted to go any farther. She had to stop for rest and food or she might faint in the middle of the Run.

When she turned to leave at the next exit, she stumbled and almost fell. She looked down to see what had caused her to trip. It was an Indian arrowhead in almost perfect condition. Minabell, who admired fine craftsmanship, stored it away in her backpack and thought no more about it.

Then she climbed the snow-covered bank and checked for traffic on Interstate 55. The coast was clear. She ran across the highway and stopped, looking out over the prairie.

Tired as Minabell was, she caught her breath at the beauty of the scene before her. The full moon shone down on the prairie, bathing it in silver. Across a small pasture stood a farmhouse, and behind it, a barn, silo, and henhouse. Nearby was a split rail fence. This was the place, she decided. She would make camp here, next to the fence.

Minabell unstrapped her backpack, took out her shovel, and removed the snow from the campsite at the foot of the fence post. She unrolled her sleeping bag on the cleared area. Then she ate one of Mrs. Cardinal's acornburgers and washed it down with a pawful of snow that melted deliciously on her tongue.

The distant hoot of a barn owl startled

her. She looked about fearfully, suddenly aware of being alone at night, far from home and friends.

She rummaged in her backpack and found her state flag, still wrapped in tissue. She attached it to its collapsible flagpole and placed it in the snow at the foot of her sleeping bag. The familiar gold eagle, embroidered on a white background, fluttered in the midnight breeze. She sighed, feeling comforted and, somehow, safer.

Minabell crawled into her sleeping bag and gazed up at the sky. She spoke softly to the North Star.

"Starlight, starbright,
First star I see tonight,
I wish I may, I wish I might,
Have the wish I wish tonight."

But before she could make a wish she had fallen asleep. Minabell dreamed she was adrift in the universe. She floated from one galaxy to another as easily as she might float down the mighty Illinois River.

She dreamed that she drifted through the Milky Way. She slid down the Big and Little Dippers and hovered over the edge of the world. She soared over towering mountains and finally came to rest on the prairie.

Suddenly Minabell became aware that the moon was disappearing. It was being blotted out by some dark and evil thing.

At this exact moment Minabell awoke and knew that something was looming over her and blotting out the reassuring light of the moon. She gave a startled cry, and the shadow covering the moon bent down and clapped a paw over her mouth.

"Do not move or make a sound," came a hoarse whisper.

5.
Murder in
the Henhouse

Minabell couldn't see her attacker. He had come upon her from behind, and she lay helpless, pinned to the ground. The only sounds were the heavy breathing of the stranger and the thumping of her own wildly beating heart.

As the dawn brightened the eastern sky, she slowly became aware of another sound. The stranger's quick intake of breath made it plain that he had heard the sound, too. Still gripping her firmly, he leaned forward and hooked his foot around her flagpole, knocking it to the ground. Then he scooted backward with Minabell until they were both out of sight, sitting behind the fence post.

"If you value your life, sit absolutely still," he whispered, his breath warm on her ear.

The tip of a blood-red sun slipped above the horizon, staining the snow before them. As the sun grew, so did the sound. Now Minabell could hear it clearly — a wild, fearsome chant, shouted in time to the beat of a drum.

A band of shaggy-furred creatures appeared, silhouetted against the sky. They marched across the prairie just a few mouse-yards away from where Minabell and her captor were hiding. They were huge rodents with long arms and yellow fangs that gleamed in the early light. A black banner fluttered over their heads. Minabell could barely make out a skull and crossbones and the words *Prairie Pirates* printed in white.

They shouted one word, over and over, as they marched: "SUNGAM! SUNGAM! SUNGAM!"

Their foul smell filled Minabell with terror. When she gasped for breath, the stranger's arms tightened around her in warning.

The chant and the drumbeat came to an abrupt end. The Prairie Pirates had arrived at the split rail fence. The leader quickly handed out gunnysacks to each member of the party.

Silently the drum and banner were laid aside. Silently the pirates dropped on all fours and slipped under the fence. And silently they crept single file across the farmer's pasture and disappeared into the henhouse, barn, and grain silo.

Seconds later Minabell heard the bawling of a milk cow and her calf. With a terrified whinny, a draft horse burst out of the barn door chased by six Prairie Pirates nipping at his legs. A shrill cackling and squawking came from the henhouse. A light went on in the upper floor of the farmhouse, and a window slammed open. A farmer, wearing pajamas, leaned out waving a shotgun.

The farmer fired a shot into the air and, almost as quickly as they had attacked the farm, the Prairie Pirates were gone.

Silently they retraced their route back across the pasture. But now they were laden down with stolen booty. The gunnysacks over their backs bulged with grain and ears of corn. And bringing up the rear, two of the raiding party dragged a large feathered object.

When they drew near the fence, Minabell saw what they were dragging. It was a dead chicken — a murdered hen. The hen's head bobbled forlornly across the stubbly field, leaving a trail of blood on the snow.

The pirates had trouble getting the hen under the fence rail. They pushed her from one side and they pulled her from the other. But all they managed to drag under were her legs and curled-up claws. They could not budge her plump body from the pasture side of the fence.

"Pluck her!" commanded the leader.

Four pirates began stripping the hen. White feathers flew in all directions. In a short time she lay plucked, naked and pink, upon the snow. Only a couple of tail feathers were left on her body, now one-fourth its former size.

Within a few minutes the chicken had been shoved and squeezed under the rail like a bag of bones. A few minutes more and it was lifted onto four husky shoulders. The head hung down, dead eyes open, staring back at the farm.

At a shouted order from their leader, the Prairie Pirates disappeared over a rise of land, trotting at double time, drum beating, and banner flying.

6.

The Secret Agent

Minabell and her captor watched the farmer lead his horse back into the barn and inspect his henhouse and silo. He came out shaking his head and trudged slowly back to the farmhouse. Only then did the stranger release Minabell. She struggled to her feet and faced him.

Before her stood a tall, white-furred weasel. He looked sternly down at Minabell and spoke in a deep, commanding voice. "I am

Secret Agent Wendell Weasel of the ISSP. Sorry about the rough handling, but there was no time to explain."

Minabell suddenly understood. "Why, of course!" she exclaimed. "You're a member of the Illinois State Ski Patrol." She was greatly relieved and assured him that she had not been hurt.

The secret agent walked over to his skis and ski poles lying in the snow a short distance from the fence. While he put on the skis, Minabell studied the wide leather belt around his waist. On it were hung the tools of his trade. She saw a bowie knife, a magnifying glass, field binoculars, and a microchip walkie-talkie.

She looked at him in admiration. With all that hardware how had he managed to sneak up on her? She was surprised that the clank of metal had not awakened her. He was a real professional.

A pile of white chicken feathers and a disagreeable smell were the only reminders that the Prairie Pirates had passed that way.

Minabell shuddered. She was truly thankful the secret agent had found her. Holy prairie fire! What if it had been the Prairie Pirates, instead!

"Who are the Prairie Pirates?" she asked the agent, forgetting her shyness. "Where did they come from? Where are they going?"

The secret agent spoke with quiet authority. "I will ask the questions, Miss." He held out his paw. "Your credentials, please."

Minabell looked puzzled.

"Quickly," he said impatiently. "I must see your identification. Time is running short."

She hastily took her purse from under her sleeping bag and started to hand it to him. He stopped her with an upheld paw.

"Remove the contents," he ordered. She obediently opened her purse and dumped everything out on the snow.

Secret Agent Weasel carefully examined each item. He did not seem too interested until he picked up the will. He read it aloud, glancing darkly at Minabell every now and again.

LAST WILL AND TESTAMENT
OF
PITTY PAT MOUSE

I, Pitty Pat Mouse, being of sound mind and body, do give and bequeath all my earthly possessions, namely, the ancestral home of the Mouse family, Mousehaven Manor, and all the contents therein, to my dearly beloved niece, and closest blood relative, Minabell Mouse. In witness thereof, I set down my paw and my seal.

Signed: _*Pitty Pat Mouse*_
Mousehaven Manor
Mousedale, Illinois

"And you are this niece — the Minabell Mouse of the will?" asked the agent.

"Yes," replied Minabell meekly.

He appeared satisfied. He turned his attention back to the objects on the ground. He frowned as he examined the photograph of Aunt Pitty Pat and Uncle Magnus in their wedding finery.

"Is there something wrong?" Minabell asked uneasily.

The agent's voice was cold. "Who are these two, and what is their exact relationship to you?"

Minabell looked at the picture. "That is my Aunt Pitty Pat and Uncle Magnus," she replied, bravely meeting his dark scowl with her soft brown eyes. "I'm on my way to Mousedale to visit them."

Secret Agent Weasel stood, lost in thought, gazing down at the photo. Finally he roused himself.

"I think, Ms. Minabell Mouse," he said, not unkindly, "you had better tell me the whole story."

7.
A Warning

"**I**— I hardly know where to begin," Minabell faltered.

The secret agent removed a small black book and a ballpoint pen from his belt pouch. "I suggest you begin at the beginning," he said.

"Well," said Minabell, "it all began two nights ago." It seemed so much longer, she thought. She cleared her throat and started again. "It all began when Gaylord brought the special delivery letter. That's Gaylord Cardinal, the Rodentville mailbird," she said and waited for the secret agent to write down the name.

Once Minabell got started she told the agent everything. She told him about the fateful letter from Uncle Magnus and of her determination to rush to Aunt Pitty Pat's bedside. She told about the snowstorm and the oak limb that had nearly buried her alive. She described how her friends had rescued her from the ruins of her house and helped her on her journey. Finally Minabell was finished, out of breath and tired, as if she had relived the last two days.

The secret agent had listened carefully, taking notes all the while. It was plain he believed her story, but he said not a word as he returned his notebook to its pouch.

Suddenly the walkie-talkie on his belt crackled into life. A voice spoke through the static. "Secret Agent Wendell Weasel, report your position. This is your commanding officer speaking."

The agent flipped a switch. "Secret Agent Wendell Weasel reporting in, sir. Position — thirty miles southwest of Chicago, County of Cook, just off Rodent Run and Interstate 55."

"Have you eyeballed the suspects?"

"Sir, suspects eyeballed at 0-600 moving rapidly in a southerly direction."

"Very good, Secret Agent Weasel. Proceed with OPERATION SUNGAM as directed." There was a static-filled pause. Then the commander came back on the air, speaking in a quiet voice. "Wendell, be careful! Over."

"I will, sir," replied the weasel. "Roger wilco. Over and out." He flipped the switch again, and the walkie-talkie was silent.

The secret agent turned to Minabell and placed a paw on her shoulder. He looked at her solemnly. "Ms. Mouse, you must give up your journey and return home as quickly as possible. You will be in grave danger if you travel southward.''

He released his hold on her shoulder. Then he leaned forward and, with the tip of his ski pole, printed a word in the snow.

Minabell slowly read the word out loud. "Sungam." She looked at the agent. "Isn't that what the Prairie Pirates were shouting?" she asked. "What does it mean?"

"Listen carefully, Ms. Mouse," said the agent. "Sungam is the secret code name for the leader of the Prairie Pirates. They're a band of Chicago rats — bloodthirsty criminals.''

Minabell caught her breath, remembering Gaylord's warning. "Chicago rats! Holy prairie fire!"

"Exactly!" the agent said. "And like a raging prairie fire they destroy everything in their path. Right now they are marching south to join their chief, Sungam. I fear for the safety of any creature who gets in their way.''

He pointed to the word he had printed in the snow. His voice was urgent. "Study this word carefully, Ms. Mouse. Then decide whether it is in your best interests to continue your journey. I strongly advise against it. But I can say no more. This is classified information."

Without another word he adjusted his snow goggles and pushed off with his ski poles. Minabell stood alone on the prairie, watching him disappear in a whoosh of powdered snow.

What a way to travel! If only she had a pair of skis, it would cut days off her traveling time. She could be in Mousedale in a few hours, for she had no intention of turning back. Secret Agent Weasel did not understand. Aunt Pitty Pat needed her. She had no choice but to go on, whatever the danger.

Minabell looked at the strange word printed in the snow. She bent down and traced it with her paw. *S-U-N-G-A-M*. The word meant nothing to her. Nevertheless, she decided to keep a sharp lookout for Chicago rats.

She collapsed the flagpole, wrapped the flag in the tissue paper, and returned them both to her backpack. Then she rolled up her sleeping bag and strapped this, also, to her backpack. She ate another of Mrs. Cardinal's acornburgers and swallowed a mouthful of snow. She was ready to travel.

But wait. There lay Teena's long, narrow Christmas package. She had almost forgotten it. She sighed. It would have to be wedged back into the straps of her backpack.

Suddenly she remembered. Just to make sure, she counted forward from the evening she had left Rodentville on December 23rd. She had been two nights and a day on the road. Twenty-three, twenty-four, twenty-five. Why, of course! It was Christmas morning!

Minabell closed her eyes and lifted her face to the heavens. A quiet sense of peace and joy descended upon her. She opened her eyes, and all around her the snow crystals glittered in the winter sun like a million tiny Christmas tree lights.

And since it was Christmas, she no longer had to carry Teena's gift. She removed the wrapping paper and sat back with a cry of surprise. The package contained a beautifully hand-carved set of skis and ski poles. Only Teena would have thought of such a gift. And only she was clever enough to make it, for she was a master woodcarver.

She remembered Teena's farewell hug and wink as she had said, "Merry Christmas, Minabell. Have a *speedy* journey."

"Merry Christmas, Teena, dearest," she whispered.

She strapped her Christmas present on her feet. Then, taking the ski poles in her paws, she pushed off just as the secret agent had done.

After a few practice slaloms and a few practice falls, she got used to skiing. Soon she was flying over the snow with the chill December wind blowing through her back-fur.

8.

A Name Revealed

"**W**heeeee!" cried Minabell as she flew before the wind.

Never before had she known the thrills of cross-country skiing. She forgot the sad nature of her journey and the dangers that might lie ahead. Wind and speed and glittering snow were what mattered, and she gave herself to the moment.

At noon she decided to stop for a rest and a bite to eat. She took off her skis and climbed up on an outcropping of rock, hoping to get a better view of the area.

She removed the state map of Illinois from her backpack and sat down to study it. Suddenly out of the corner of her eye she caught a movement below her in the shadow of the rock.

In the next instant two large, gray farm cats leaped together over the edge of the rock into the sunlight. The larger cat sailed right over the top of the boulder. He spun around in midair and landed facing Minabell. Before she had a chance to recover, the other cat came down squarely on top of her and the map. She was smashed into the rock by a brutish paw and knocked unconscious.

When she regained her senses she found herself airborne. She was being tossed like a plaything from one cat to the other.

As Minabell flew back and forth through the air, she grew angrier and angrier. She was so outraged she didn't think of the dangers of her situation. She only wanted to show these bullies she wasn't going to take any more of their abuse.

As Minabell sprawled in front of the grinning cat on top of the rock, she took careful aim and landed a sharp uppercut to his gaping jaw. With a snarl he tossed her back to the cat on the ground. Minabell reared back from this second creature and connected with a hard karate kick to the nose. At the same time she shouted an insult into his smirking face. And the word that came tumbling out was the ugliest word she could think of in the heat of the moment. It was the word that had been troubling her ever since Agent Wendell Weasel had left.

"SUNGAM!" she screamed, waving her arms in front of the cat's startled eyes.

Gray fur standing on end, he spat and hissed at Minabell as if she had changed into a mad dog. The other cat arched his back in fright and sprang, caterwauling, off the rock.

Minabell sighed with relief as she watched her former luncheon companions disappear over the snow. Exhausted, she collapsed at the base of the rock and found to her surprise that she was unhurt. Actually it was her feelings that had been bruised, not her body. She did not appreciate being bullied. A sense of her own inner dignity had been grossly violated.

While Minabell sat resting, a faint worry began nibbling at the edges of her mind. She tried to dismiss it. She wanted only to sit dreaming in the sunlight for yet a while. But the thought wouldn't go away. It tugged at her until she sat upright with an uneasy sigh and gave it her full attention.

Sungam! That was what was bothering her. Just the sound of this word had sent the farm cats fleeing in terror. She suddenly felt chilled. Why had Wendell Weasel insisted she study the name of the Prairie Pirates' leader before continuing her journey to Mousehaven Manor?

She leaned forward and idly wrote *S-U-N-G-A-M*

in the snow. Then slowly, hardly realizing
what she was doing, she wrote it out again —
backwards. And the word that appeared under her shaking paw was
   M-A-G-N-U-S!

9.
The Skull
and Crossbones

Minabell took a deep breath of the cold air and tried to remain calm. She had broken the secret code name of the leader of the Prairie Pirates. It could be none other than Uncle Magnus.

The agent had recognized him in the wedding picture and tried to warn her.

She must compose herself and consider what to do. Should she return to Rodentville and safety, as the agent had suggested? Or should she continue her journey?

It was the afternoon sun that finally decided Minabell on a course of action. The lengthening shadows warned her that the hour was late, and she had lingered too long.

Aunt Pitty Pat was waiting for her. She would continue on to Mousedale.

She quickly retrieved her map and strapped on her backpack. Then, slipping into her skis, she once more set out upon her journey. A strong tail wind soon had her flying effortlessly southward.

As the landscape flashed by, Minabell had time to think. Three points soon became clear to her.

Point number one: Some grave peril threatened her beloved prairie, and Uncle Magnus was involved.

The very thought made her stumble. It was with great effort that she forced herself to continue skiing and think about the next point.

Point number two: The murderers, calling themselves the Prairie Pirates, had last been seen heading south. The agent had said they were going to meet their leader, Sungam. This could only mean one thing. They were on their way to Mousedale to join Magnus at Mousehaven Manor.

"Oh, dear!" she wailed. "Aunt Pitty Pat!" Minabell prayed that she would arrive before they did. Then she hastily went on to the third point.

Point number three: Secret Agent Weasel, ISSP, had been put in charge of the case. Of this, too, she was certain. She clearly remembered the words of his superior officer — "Proceed with OPERATION SUNGAM."

Minabell took some comfort from point number three. But she wondered how one secret agent could possibly stop the vicious mob that had attacked the farm.

She shook her head in frustration. It was all too much for her. And since she could find no answers to her questions, she concentrated on her skiing.

The mousemiles flew by, and the shadows continued to lengthen as the afternoon sun hurried to meet the horizon. Finally Minabell's long journey came to an end.

Minabell's skis kicked up a spray of powdered snow as she skidded to an abrupt stop on a hilltop overlooking the village of Mousedale. Breathless, she gazed down at her ancestral home.

She knew at once which building was Mousehaven Manor. It stood on a rise of land in the center of the village, dominating the scene before her. How beautiful it was! The manor, completely built of prairie pebbles, shimmered in the twilight. The glow from the setting sun revealed a rainbow of colors locked within the ancient walls.

She carefully studied the stately old mansion. In front of the manor stood a large statue. It appeared to be a figure carved out of stone, holding a flagpole in one paw. Should she ski down the hill, past the statue, right up to the main entrance and demand to see Aunt Pitty Pat? Or would it be wiser to approach more cautiously?

Suddenly the lights went on, one by one, in the manor. The front door opened, and a large rodent came out, carrying a black flag. He trotted over to the statue and jumped up on the pedestal. He climbed paw over paw up the flagpole and attached the flag to the top of the pole.

Minabell watched as the black flag slowly unfurled in the evening breeze — revealing a skull and crossbones!

10.
The Cave

Minabell glanced nervously about, suddenly aware of her dangerous position on the hillside. Had the Prairie Pirates posted guards? Had she been seen?

But all was quiet under the rising moon. No shadow moved. No menacing figure appeared out of the dusk. She was alone on the hillside.

Greatly relieved, Minabell removed her skis and looked around for a place to hide them. They might be needed for a quick getaway. She found what she was looking for at the base of a large boulder. It was a narrow crevice opening into a warm, dry chamber. This would make an ideal spot to store her belongings.

She took off her gear and backed through the entrance, pulling the skis and backpack in after her. Fumbling in her purse, she found her flashlight and examined the shelter.

It was a large cave with a high ceiling, jutting stone ledges, and a clean, sandy floor. Minabell looked about the room with a feeling of satisfaction. For the first time since leaving Secret Agent Weasel, she felt safe. She set the flashlight on a ledge and directed its beam out into the room. Then she sat down on the floor and tried to think of what to do next.

"Caution is the better part of valor," she lectured herself. "Forewarned is forearmed," was another useful saying that came to mind. But neither of these proverbs offered much comfort.

Then Minabell recalled a favorite mouse-maxim of her aunt's. It was one that had been of great help to her in other times of stress. She could almost hear Aunt Pitty Pat's cheerful voice:

"Brushing fur
And whiskers may
Embolden spirits
And ease the way."

"Of course!" said Minabell firmly. "First things first."

She rummaged in her purse and came up with a mirror, brush, and comb. She also took out a pair of clean white mittens. Come what may, she intended to look her best for Aunt Pitty Pat's sake.

Using the mirror, she gave close attention to the grooming of her tail. Then she brushed her white breast-fur until it glistened. A quick comb-out of her face-whiskers, and she was finished.

As usual after applying the good advice of her wise little aunt, Minabell felt better. She was still uncertain about how to approach the evil in the valley. But now she felt equal to the challenge.

Minabell put on the fresh white mittens

and, with a deep sigh of regret, prepared to leave her hideaway. Before going, she stood for some moments holding her aunt's last will and testament. Should she bring it with her as Uncle Magnus had insisted? Then she remembered that Magnus was also Sungam. She decided to leave the will in the cave until she had met her uncle and knew more about his intentions. She replaced it in her back-pack.

Standing in the center of the cave, she closed her eyes, turned around three times and recited the mouse's ancient Remember-ing Rhyme:

> "Three times I twirl
> For rodent luck.
> Three times I twirl
> With rodent pluck.
> I'll never reveal
> This secret space.
> I'll never forget
> This hiding place."

Then with her eyes still shut she performed the Magic Brow-Writing Trick. She started to write the word *B-O-U-L-D-E-R* on her forehead. But halfway across she realized the word was too long to fit. So she erased it and wrote *R-O-C-K* instead.

With a final look around, Minabell turned off the flashlight and slipped out of the narrow entryway. She hesitated only a moment. Then, trying not to think of what might be waiting for her, she descended into the valley.

11.
Uncle Magnus

When Minabell reached the bottom of the hill her nose got a sudden whiff of a familiar stench. It smelled like rotten eggs just cracked open.

"Holy Prairie Fire!" she muttered under her breath and quickly covered her nose. There was no doubt about it. The Prairie Pirates had arrived and settled in.

She entered the outskirts of the village and slowly made her way through the deserted streets. No friendly glow shone from the cottage windows to light her way. All the curtains were drawn, and the village appeared to be abandoned.

Yet Minabell felt eyes watching her progress through the narrow cobbled streets. She heard faint whispers behind the closed doors and shuttered windows. And there was the occasional cry of a young one, quickly hushed.

Once, looking back, she caught a glimpse

73

of a curtain being pushed aside and a small, pointed face peering out at her from a darkened window. Then the curtain dropped back in place, and the face disappeared.

Minabell came to the end of the street and stopped. She looked out over the snow-covered park that separated her from Mousehaven Manor. The great house was ablaze with lights. Just then the front door was flung open, and the light and noise streamed out into the night. She ducked behind a cottage wall.

A Prairie Pirate staggered through the entrance. He stumbled across the park and disappeared down an alley on her left. Harsh laughter and wild music came from the open doorway. Then the door slammed shut, and she was in the dark again. But now she was not alone. The pirate was somewhere behind her, down the alley. She was afraid to step forward into the moonlight and be seen, and afraid to go back the way she had come.

Then she noticed the monument she had seen from the hillside. It loomed up in the center of the park, midway between the manor and the cottage wall where she was hiding. It was a statue of a rodent carved from prairie stone and set on a rectangular base.

Two torches, one on each side of the manor's entrance, lit the back of the monument. The front of the statue, facing Minabell, was in darkness. It cast a long shadow that stretched almost to where she was standing.

Before she could change her mind, she crept forward into the shadow and ran quickly along its length to the base of the monument. Breathless, she pressed against the stone. She had not been seen. She relaxed and looked up at the statue towering above her.

It was a huge figure of a mouse. One paw shielded his eyes as he gazed over the town to the prairie beyond. The other paw held the flagpole flying the skull and crossbones.

Minabell touched the letters carved into the base. She spelled out the name under her breath — "Geronimouse." It was a statue of the famous pioneer mouse of olden days who had built Rodent Run. He had also founded Mousedale and built Mousehaven Manor. She recalled the old mousetales of how he had defended the village and the mansion against all attacks.

A sudden shouted curse from a manor window snapped Minabell to attention. She could not stay here. She stood up in the shadow of Geronimouse, determined to be a credit to her famous ancestor.

She took a firm grip on her purse, and a firmer grip on her courage, and stepped out from behind the statue. A few steps more and she stood exposed in the torchlight.

She gave a startled cry as a guard appeared out of the dark to the right of the manor's entrance.

"Stand and be recognized!" he growled.

Minabell held her head high and stood as straight and tall as she could. "I am Ms. Minabell Mouse," she said with just the barest quiver in her voice. "I have come to visit my aunt and uncle, Mr. and Mrs. Magnus Mouse — Rat — er, that is — " She stopped in confusion, uncertain of what to call her aunt and uncle.

The evil-looking rodent leaned down and peered into her face with small, bloodshot eyes. Minabell took a nervous step backward in a vain attempt to escape his foul breath.

"So you're the one," he said, his voice harsh. "Too puny for my taste. Not enough meat on your bones." He guffawed loudly and waved a paw at the door. "Go on in. He's waiting for you."

The guard stepped back into the darkness, and Minabell was left alone in front of the door. She squared her shoulders and lifted the latch. She slowly pushed the door open and stepped into a brightly lit foyer.

She stood in the entryway, which opened into a great hall several stories high. A grand staircase curved upward to the floors above. The floor of the hall was strewn with broken furniture and debris. On either side of the hall were rooms from which the shouts and din of rat merrymaking could be heard. The crystal chandelier over her head tinkled in protest.

A door opened on the right, and unseen paws threw a pail of slop on top of the garbage already piled on the floor.

Minabell jumped as a roar issued from

the room. The noise in all the other rooms immediately stopped.

"GREAT LEAPING CATFISH!" bellowed a voice into the sudden silence. "Can't I get anything to eat around here but greens and nuts? Mouse food — BLAH! Where's that chicken the raiding party brought in?"

There was a clatter as if someone had thrown a dish of greens and a frightened squeal as the dish obviously hit its target.

"I want chicken," bawled the voice. "Bring me a chicken leg, you stupid rodent, or I'll have *you* on a platter for supper!"

Minabell stood rooted to the floor as she heard a chair being scraped back from a table and heavy footsteps shuffling toward the door.

A moment later a huge, potbellied rat filled the doorway. He lounged lazily against the door frame, picking his yellow fangs with one of Aunt Pitty Pat's knitting needles. He gazed down at Minabell with small, close-set eyes.

On either side of the hall the doors opened, and the room was soon crowded with rats, staring at Minabell.

The large rat in the doorway took the knitting needle from his mouth and placed it daintily behind an ear, never taking his eyes from his guest. He spoke softly. "Ms. Minabell Mouse, I presume? What an unexpected pleasure."

An answer seemed to be called for. But Minabell had forgotten her mousemanners.

The rat smiled down at her. "Cat got our tongue?" he inquired.

He moved from the doorway. "Give your Uncle Magnus a kiss," he said with a leer, lunging at her.

Minabell regained her voice and, with a frightened squeal, darted behind an over-turned chair.

"Shy, are we? Now that's what I like to see in a proper young female mouse."

Minabell shuddered. She recognized him now from the wedding picture. How could she ever have mistaken this great, ugly rat for a mouse?

They stood facing each other over the upended chair. Clutching her purse, Minabell waited, ready to jump out of his reach. But he was too fast for her. Without warning his arm shot out and he lifted her bodily over the chair.

He held her pinned against his greasy

belly and stared with crafty eyes into her terrified face. "Where is it?" he demanded.

"Where is what?" she managed to whisper. He was holding her so tightly she could hardly breathe.

"Where is the will? Did you bring the old hag's will?" His eyes shifted to her purse and, with his free paw, he yanked it from her arm. He tossed Minabell to the nearest pirate. "Hold on to her, Number Two."

He opened the purse and pawed through it. When he couldn't find the will, he snarled in disgust and threw the purse on the floor. Minabell watched her comb and brush tumble out and join the filth.

"You might as well tell me where it is, my little miss," said Magnus. "We have ways to make you talk."

As if to prove this point, Number Two gave her a sharp squeeze. She gasped and tears of pain welled up in her eyes. But she didn't give him the satisfaction of hearing her cry out.

The front door opened, and the guard stuck his head in. "There's a big red bird out here," he said.

"Grab him," said Magnus. "We can use some red meat in the stew pot."

"He looks sort of tough and stringy to me. He says Minabell Mouse is his friend. He wants to talk to her."

At the mention of her name, Minabell gave a startled cry. "Gaylord Cardinal!" Number Two silenced her with a paw over her mouth.

Magnus looked at Minabell. "A friend of yours?" he asked kindly. His manner abruptly changed. "Get her out of sight, Number Two," he commanded. "And keep her quiet," he added rather needlessly, Minabell thought, from behind the big paw covering her face.

Magnus waited until Number Two hid behind a door with his prisoner. He nodded to the guard. "Bring this bird in, and let's have a look at him."

12.
The Dungeon

Minabell squirmed in Number Two's grasp as she tried to see into the hall from behind the door. Finally she managed to get a clear view through the crack. While they waited, she counted the Prairie Pirates lounging around the room. There were forty-nine of them —fifty, counting the smelly brute who held her. Magnus stood facing the entrance, paws on hips, impatiently awaiting their visitor.

The front door opened, and the guard shoved Gaylord Cardinal into the foyer. Legs stiffly braced, he skidded in on the slop and came to an abrupt stop in front of Magnus.

Gaylord stood blinking in the bright lights. He delicately lifted one claw and then the other out of the unpleasant mess on the floor.

Magnus walked around the cardinal, inspecting him from beak to tail.

"How is your dark meat?" he inquired sociably. He leaned over and pinched Gaylord's thigh. "Hmmm. Sort of scrawny, aren't we?"

Gaylord flapped his wings and squawked. "Unpaw me, sir! How dare you molest the state bird of Illinois?"

Magnus sneered. "Did you hear that, pirates? We have a special visitor, a V.I.B. — Very Important Bird." He bowed low in front of Gaylord.

Hoots and birdcalls filled the room as the Prairie Pirates made fun of the cardinal.

Behind the door Minabell watched fearfully. Dear, foolish Gaylord. His headcrest was quivering, and she knew he was frightened. But he bravely strutted about the room lecturing the rowdy crowd.

"I, sirs, am your state bird. Harm me and it won't be long before you are trampling your state flower. For shame! What will be next? Dragging your state flag through the mud?"

"SHUT UP!" Magnus roared.

Gaylord's beak snapped shut.

"Big bird," said Magnus, "since you're a friend of Minabell Mouse, maybe you know where she has hidden the will?"

"I know nothing about a will, sir." Gaylord puffed out his breast feathers. "I have come to call on Ms. Minabell Mouse and pay my respects to her ailing aunt."

"String the windbag up," shouted a pirate.

The cry was taken up by the others. "String him up! String him up!"

Gaylord turned on his attackers. "Be careful," he warned. "My comrades are waiting for me. I have come with a full company of the Illinois State Ski Patrol. If I am harmed it will go badly for all of you."

At the mention of the ISSP, the shouting died down. In the silence that followed, Magnus issued an order. "Tie him up!"

Several pirates pounced on Gaylord and pinned him to the floor. Someone produced a rope and tied his wings behind his back. Someone else bound his claws together. Within seconds Gaylord lay helpless. His only movable part was his beak.

"Help!" he squawked.

"Silence him," yelled Magnus, and Gaylord's beak was taped shut.

Magnus sent his cutthroats out into the night with orders to guard all the entrances to the manor and to capture anything that moved.

He ordered three of the biggest pirates to stay behind as a rear guard. Two of them picked up Gaylord, and Minabell was brought out of hiding. Gaylord gazed at her in mute distress.

Number Two put Minabell down for a moment while he recovered his weapon, a dangerous-looking spiked club. Minabell just had time to snatch up her purse from the floor and toss in her comb and brush. Then she was roughly picked up again. Magnus led the way, holding a lighted torch, as they were carried down the hallway.

They went through a small door under the staircase and descended several flights. Number Two carried Minabell upside down under his arm. She could see nothing but the stone floor beneath her and the hairy feet of the Prairie Pirate in front of her. But the delicious smell of dried herbs and fruit told her they were passing through Mousehaven Manor's root cellar.

They went down another flight of stairs and stopped in front of a heavy oaken door. Magnus removed the padlock, and the door slowly swung open on rusty hinges. Minabell had no time to observe her surroundings. Number Two tied her up paw and foot and threw her into a dark corner. Magnus tied a long rope around Gaylord's claws and strung him upside down from the rafters.

The pirates trotted out of the dungeon with Magnus bringing up the rear. He turned at the door and looked at Minabell. "I'm going to get rid of the ISSP," he snarled. "Then I'll be back. You had better be prepared to tell me the whereabouts of that will, my dear niece." The heavy door slammed shut, the padlock rattled into place, and Minabell and Gaylord were left in the dark.

Minabell lay on the damp, cobbled floor, straining to undo her bindings. She could hear the sound of water dripping and Gaylord's strangled squawks as he tried to free himself.

She leaned forward into the blackness, listening. What was that?

"Be quiet, Gaylord," she whispered. "I think I hear something."

The steady drip, drip, drip of water filled the silence. And then they both heard it.

From the far side of the dungeon came a feeble cry.

"Someone is in here with us," Minabell whispered. She raised her voice. "Who's there?"

For answer there was another cry, stronger this time.

"Who are you?" Minabell called out. "Are you able to speak? Can you move?"

There was a long, muffled wail, plainly in the negative. Whoever it was must be bound and gagged.

Minabell had a sudden inspiration. "I'm going to roll over to you. Keep calling out so I can find you." A few minutes later she bumped against a softly furred body lying against the far wall. "Hold out your paws," she said. "I'll try to gnaw the ropes."

In a short while the bindings fell away, and the gag was removed. "Land sakes, Minabell, is that you?" whispered a familiar voice.

Minabell peered uncertainly into the dark. "Aunt Pitty Pat?"

"It's me, mouseling," murmured her aunt. With fumbling paws Aunt Pitty Pat untied Minabell's ropes, and they fell into each other's arms.

Minabell sat back. "Aunt Pitty Pat! I thought you were sick. What are you doing down here, bound and gagged, a prisoner in your own manor?"

13.
Aunt Pitty Pat's Story

*T*hey were interrupted by frantic squawks from the ceiling.

"Gaylord!" In the excitement of finding her aunt, Minabell had forgotten the mailbird. He was still hanging upside down from the rafters, his beak taped shut. "Hold on," she said. "I'll have you down in no time."

She groped her way across the damp floor, searching in the dark for her purse. She finally found it near the door and removed her flashlight.

She set the flashlight on the floor and, in its dim light, glanced quickly at Aunt Pitty Pat. Her usually neat and tidy aunt sat forlornly against the wall, side-whiskers drooping, breast-fur unkempt. But she managed a brave little smile.

There were strangled protests from the ceiling again. "I'm coming, Gaylord," Minabell said. She ran to the rope and untied it from the peg by which the cardinal had been raised, pulley fashion, to the oak beam. Using all her strength she carefully lowered him to the floor. Then she untied his bindings, removed the tape from his beak, and smoothed his ruffled feathers.

Gaylord stood up and stretched his legs. He was about to thank Minabell, when there came a faint cry from the other side of the dungeon.

Aunt Pitty Pat still sat propped against the wall. As they watched, she slid sideways and lay in a crumpled heap on the cobblestones. "Water," she whispered.

Minabell ran across the room and gathered her aunt in her arms. Gaylord hovered over them, flapping his wings in distress.

"Quickly, Gaylord," Minabell said. "There's a handkerchief in my purse. Dampen it with some of the water dripping from the walls."

The mailbird flew into action. He soon had the handkerchief soaking wet and was wringing a steady stream of water into Aunt Pitty Pat's mouth.

She struggled to a sitting position, gasping for breath. "That's enough, Gaylord," she said, waving him away. "Land sakes! I do believe you're trying to drown me." She laughed weakly. Suddenly they were all holding their sides, doubled over, helpless with laughter.

Aunt Pitty Pat was the first to recover. She daintily wiped her eyes on the back of a paw. Then she took a deep breath and recited a rodent rhyme befitting the occasion.

"Frolic and laughter
Never fail
To increase the starch
In a rodent's tail."

Minabell clapped her paws. "I know you're

feeling better when you start reciting mouse-maxims, Aunt Pitty Pat."

"I am feeling better," admitted her aunt. "But I'm still a bit faint. I haven't had anything to eat or drink for two days."

Minabell rummaged around in the bottom of her purse and triumphantly held up the last of the acornburgers. While Aunt Pitty Pat ate, Minabell brushed out her matted fur.

Finally, much refreshed, Aunt Pitty Pat leaned back against the wall with a sigh of contentment.

Minabell took her aunt's little paw in hers and looked at her gravely. "Aunt Pitty Pat, we were so worried about you. We all thought you were ill. Tell us what's happened. We don't have much time. Uncle Magnus will be back soon."

At the mention of Magnus, Aunt Pitty Pat trembled with indignation. "*Uncle* Magnus, indeed! That loathsome creature is not my husband and is, most certainly, not your uncle."

At Minabell's look of relieved surprise she said spiritedly: "I would never marry such a miserable rat — and a Chicago rat, at that."

With great effort Aunt Pitty Pat composed herself. "As you can see, mouseling, I'm not ailing. I'm just a bit weak from lack of food. Magnus wrote you that I was ill to lure you to Mousehaven Manor. And I couldn't stop him."

She suddenly sat up straight and twitched her side-whiskers. "You're right, Minabell. Time is running out. I must tell you the whole story as quickly as possible. Magnus and the Prairie Pirates have to be stopped, or not a mouse or creature in the state will be safe."

They huddled close together, and Aunt Pitty Pat closed her eyes in thought. "It all began on the night Magnus and three of his gang came to the manor asking for food and shelter. They said they were poor wayfaring mice, traveling westward."

"A likely story," squawked Gaylord. He

jumped to his claws and paced angrily back and forth.

"Gaylord, please!" entreated Minabell.

He sat back down on the cobblestones, and Aunt Pitty Pat continued. "I took pity on them and invited them to stay the night. Mousehaven Manor never turns away rodents in need of shelter." She shuddered. "But this time it would have been wiser if I had."

She paused and then spoke in a low but firm voice. "That very night they attacked me while I slept and bound me to my bed."

"The scoundrels!" screamed Gaylord. He jumped up, flailing the air with his wings. "Take that! And that — you rats!" He danced across the room, shadowboxing with an imagined foe.

Minabell sighed. "Do sit down, Gaylord."

"Sorry," he muttered.

"Go on, Aunt Pitty Pat," urged Minabell. "What happened?"

"Magnus and his pirates wanted my will, mouseling. That's what they had come for. All through the night they ransacked the manor looking for it. They intended to destroy it and, with it, your inheritance."

"But Aunt Pitty Pat, why does Magnus need the will? He already has what he wants. He's taken the manor by force."

Aunt Pitty Pat leaned closer, her voice trembling. "I overheard Magnus and Number Two talking. They are planning to lead all Chicago rats — thousands of them — in a takeover of the entire state of Illinois. Mousehaven Manor is to be their headquarters. And they don't want any trouble with the law until Magnus is the legal owner of the manor. They didn't know I'd given the will to you."

"How did they find out? I'd almost forgotten I had it, myself."

"I'm afraid, mouseling, I made a foolish mistake. I told them my niece had the will. But when I refused to tell them where you lived, they asked questions in town. They soon found out you were living in Rodent-ville."

She leaned back wearily. "That's when Magnus hatched his plan. He decided to trick you into bringing the will to Mousehaven. As soon as he gets his paws on it he's planning to kill us both. Then he'll announce himself the new owner and make out a new will to prove it."

"Holy prairie fire!"

Aunt Pitty Pat looked anxiously at her niece. "I hope you haven't brought the will with you." When Minabell told of hiding it under a boulder on the hilltop, her aunt sighed with relief. "That's Indian Mound Hill. It'll be safe there."

Minabell remembered her pleasure in the warmth and safety of the cave. "Indian Mound Hill. So that's what it's called."

"It's an old Indian burial site," said her aunt. "But that historical fact won't help us when Magnus returns." She stared at Minabell with frightened eyes. "Oh, mouseling, what will we do?"

14.
All Hope Lost

*A*unt Pitty Pat heaved a great sigh. "If only we could get word to the Illinois State Ski Patrol." At the mention of the ISSP Gaylord jumped to his claws.

"Aunt Pitty Pat! I'd almost forgotten. I came to Mousehaven Manor with a rescue party."

"I'd forgotten, too," cried Minabell, hugging her aunt. "Gaylord brought a company of the ISSP with him." She turned to the cardinal. "Did Wendell Weasel come with you?"

"Yes, Minabell — but . . . " Gaylord's crest fell, and he dropped his wings to his sides.

"What is it, Gaylord? Is there something you haven't told us?"

"I'm afraid so, Minabell. The truth is — I didn't bring the ISSP. There are only five of us. I came with the secret agent, Teena Chipmunk, Mumbles Mole, and Mrs. Cardinal."

Gaylord stopped talking and cocked his head, listening. Then they all heard the sound of approaching footsteps. There was a rattle of keys outside the dungeon door.

"Quickly!" whispered Minabell. "Get back to your positions." She turned off the flashlight and darted across to the wall. She lay down, with her paws behind her back, as if they were bound. Aunt Pitty Pat did the same. Gaylord flew up to the ceiling and clung upside down from the rafters, holding the end of the rope in his claws.

The door creaked open, and a pirate stood in the threshold, carrying a lantern. For a long, silent moment he peered in at them. Satisfied, he withdrew, closing the heavy door behind him. They listened to the padlock falling into place and to his feet padding back down the corridor.

"Phew!" Minabell let out her breath. "Gaylord," she whispered, "come down and finish telling us what happened to the ISSP."

Gaylord fluttered down from the ceiling. He paced back and forth, his voice low and hurried. "This morning Wendell Weasel arrived in Rodentville. He told of meeting you on the prairie and warning you not to travel to Mousedale. He said you hadn't listened to him and were in great danger."

"My place was by Aunt Pitty Pat's side," Minabell said quietly.

"Well," said the cardinal, "volunteers were needed to rescue you and your aunt. So, of course, your friends agreed to help."

"Why didn't Wendell Weasel call his commanding officer on his walkie-talkie and ask for help?" asked Minabell.

Gaylord's voice was mournful. "He did call for help. But he was told that all ISSP troops had been sent to Peoria. The Prairie Pirates had burned the town granary to the ground. Every able-bodied agent was needed to help evacuate the mice families living in the granary and guard against looting by the pirates."

Gaylord paused to catch his breath. "So here I am, Minabell. I left the rest of the rescue party on Indian Mound Hill. I was sent ahead to scout the area and report back your position. But I was captured before I could carry out my task."

"How did you all arrive from Rodentville so quickly? I had two days' head start. But you must have arrived on the hill soon after I left it."

"The secret agent hired two prairie hawks," said the mailbird. "It's only a half day's journey by air. Teena and Mumbles rode on one hawk, and the agent rode on the other. Mrs. Cardinal and I, of course, flew in on our own wing power."

"I see," Minabell said. And she did see now, only too clearly. What could the agent and a rescue party of four do against an army of fifty rats? Without the ISSP it was hopeless. "I'm afraid we're outnumbered, Gaylord."

For once, Gaylord had nothing to say. With a despairing shrug of his wings, he slumped to the floor. Minabell and Aunt Pitty Pat sat down close to him, and the cold closed in upon them.

15.

An Old Ballad

"**M**inabell," said Aunt Pitty Pat, "our friends from Rodentville are going to rescue us. I just *know* they are."

She jumped to her feet and stood facing them, shoulders back, paws clasped in front of her. She was, once again, the high-spirited and cheerful mouse Minabell had always known. She lifted her head, twitched her side-whiskers, and began to sing. Her sweet voice floated to the rafters, filling the dungeon with joyous song.

"Mousehaven stories
Oft are told
Of companions true
Staunch-hearted, bold.

Mousehaven tales
Of a mouse's pleasure
In friendship given
In fullest measure.

Paws that tilt
The dungeon stone
Are paws that clasp
In friendship grown."

Minabell had heard this song many times since she had been a mouseling in arms. She had always thought it was a song of friendship. But now she was not so sure. It had suddenly taken on new meaning. And she was desperate enough to grab at any straw.

She interrupted Gaylord. He was clapping his wingtips and shouting, "Bravo!" as he urged Aunt Pitty Pat to sing another ballad. Minabell questioned her aunt closely about the exact meaning of the song, especially the third verse.

"Now that I think about it," said Aunt Pitty Pat, "the third stanza is puzzling."

"Paws that tilt the dungeon stone," Minabell said slowly. "I wonder what that means? Is it some kind of secret code?" She jumped to her feet. "Holy prairie fire! Maybe there is a way out of this dungeon besides the door. Maybe there's a hidden panel in the wall." She looked with bright, expectant eyes at Aunt Pitty Pat. "Perhaps tilting the dungeon stone will open it."

Her aunt looked doubtful. "I don't think so, Minabell. I've never heard of any hidden panels down here. There was once said to be an underground passageway beneath Mousehaven Manor. But that's only gossip. Just another foolish rodent rumor."

Gaylord sighed. "Farewell, vast rolling prairies! Farewell, Olivia, my beloved wife! I shall never behold thy fair feathers again."

"Of one thing I am positive," said Aunt Pitty Pat briskly, "it must be *this dungeon* that is mentioned in the song. It's the only dungeon in the manor."

"In that case," Minabell said, "if there is a special dungeon stone, it has to be right here within paw's reach." She looked at the pebbled walls. "Oh, dear. There are so many stones. It could be any one of them."

Gaylord glowered. "Or none of them," he muttered.

"We'll never know unless we start looking," Minabell said.

A half hour later they had found nothing but mouse masonry. One pebble fitted neatly next to another without a break of any kind. And none of them could be moved or tilted. Aunt Pitty Pat and Gaylord had stopped their search. Discouraged, they watched Minabell examine a corner section of wall.

"Give it up, mouseling," urged Aunt Pitty Pat. "I'm afraid there is no secret dungeon stone, no hidden passageway."

Minabell decided her aunt was probably right, and she was about to turn away when she noticed something waist high, half hidden in the shadows. It was a shallow, well-worn ledge that appeared to have been deliberately made. It could be a foothold, Minabell decided. But why would anyone build a foothold in the wall? She called to her companions, and they ran over to inspect it.

It had never occurred to them to look higher. Now Gaylord flew up and examined the wall above the ledge. To the left, about mouse-high if one were standing on the ledge, he found a small, round opening. Using a trick he learned from a hummingbird friend, he rapidly fluttered his wings and hovered at the site. He placed an eye to the opening and announced, with a squawk of triumph, that he could see a small object in the back of the hole.

"Gaylord, look!" Minabell pointed over her head. "Here's another hole on this side of the ledge."

Gaylord flew to the other side and looked in the second opening. "I see it!" he yelled. "There's something in the back of this hole, too." In his excitement he forgot to hover and fell to the floor with a resounding thump. The wind was knocked out of him, and he lay still a moment catching his breath.

As soon as he recovered, he jumped to his claws to help Minabell, who was trying to climb up on the narrow ledge. With a boost from Gaylord, she managed to gain a footing and stand upright.

Aunt Pitty Pat stood below, anxiously watching. "Be careful, Minabell."

Pressed against the wall, holding on with her right paw, Minabell slowly worked her other paw across the pebbles toward the hole on the left. When she touched the rim of the opening, she stopped and took a deep breath. Then she moved her paw into the opening and carefully felt around.

Aunt Pitty Pat and Gaylord held their breath, not knowing what to expect.

"What is it, Minabell? What's in there?" Gaylord asked.

"It's a small, smooth stone fitted into the back of the hole." Minabell's voice was muffled by the wall. "This could be the dungeon stone — or one of them. There must be one in the other opening, too."

"But the song mentions only one stone," Gaylord pointed out.

"Poetic license," murmured Aunt Pitty Pat.

"What are you going to do?" asked Gaylord.

"I'm going to do what it says in the song. I'm going to tilt the dungeon stone," Minabell said. "Stand back from the wall." Aunt Pitty Pat and Gaylord moved away.

"There!" muttered Minabell as she pressed the stone and felt it move inward. But nothing happened. No hidden panel magically opened. No secret passageway was suddenly revealed. They sighed in disappointment.

Minabell had an idea. "Gaylord, try to

tilt the stone in the other hole. Perhaps if we do it together something will happen."

Gaylord fluttered up and attempted to insert his beak into the other opening. But he wasn't able to hover long enough. He kept losing altitude and falling back.

"Let me try." Aunt Pitty Pat scrambled up on the ledge and stood next to Minabell, facing the wall.

They watched as she repeated the steps Minabell had taken, but in the opposite direction. Clinging to the wall with her left paw, she inched her right paw slowly across the pebbles toward the hole on her side. But her arm wasn't long enough. She couldn't reach it.

"Now what?" asked Gaylord.

"Paws that clasp in friendship grown," recited Minabell. "Aunt Pitty Pat, if we both let go of the wall with one paw and hold on to each other, you should be able to stretch farther and reach the hole."

"But we'll fall if we let go."

"Not if Gaylord holds us up."

"That's right," Gaylord said eagerly.

He flew up and hovered behind them, pinning them both to the wall with outstretched wings, but he kept slipping down. Finally, with a great flapping and fluttering, he managed to stay in position.

"How's that, Minabell?"

"Very good, Gaylord. Whatever happens, don't let go." Minabell took her right paw from the wall and tightly clasped her aunt's

left paw. Immediately their full weight fell back on Gaylord, and he grunted and strained as he held them in place.

Now Aunt Pitty Pat was able to stretch an extra paw's length to the right and insert her paw in the hole. A moment later she cried out, "I can feel the dungeon stone!"

When they both had their paws securely in place, Gaylord shouted, "All together now! One, two, three, TILT!"

From inside the wall came a mighty rumbling, as if a hundred pebbles were grinding, one upon the other. Suddenly the section of the wall they were clinging to swung inward like a drawbridge, and they were tumbled off into a small chamber. But there was no time to look around. The moment their weight was removed from the wall, it swung back up into place.

16.
The Belfry Tower

Minabell stood up, stretched out her paws in the dark, and touched pebbled walls on both sides. They seemed to be in a narrow passageway. "I don't think we're free yet," she whispered.

A low, damp ceiling pressed down upon them, and cold water dripped on their heads. Minabell shivered, teeth chattering. She longed for the warmth of her own snug hearth in Rodentville and for the feel of her rocking chair under her.

There was a squawk from Gaylord. "Can't we move, Minabell? This water will ruin my headcrest," complained the big bird.

Minabell sighed. "Holy prairie fire, it's so dark in here! And I left the flashlight on the other side of the dungeon wall."

"What shall we do, mouseling?" wailed Aunt Pitty Pat.

Surely, thought Minabell, we haven't come this far to be stopped for want of a little light. She took a deep breath. "Hold on to my back-fur, Aunt Pitty Pat. Gaylord, hold on to Aunt Pitty Pat. We don't want to become separated." She reached out her paws to the side walls and started inching forward.

Slowly and hesitantly, sloshing through puddles, they advanced down the passageway. Gaylord, bringing up the rear, groaned each time his soggy topknot scraped the ceiling.

At first the corridor's many twists and turns made progress difficult. But after a short distance the passageway straightened out, and they were able to move more rapidly. The air, which had been stale and musty, began to freshen. A few minutes later,

Minabell was struck by a cool breeze that had the hint of snow in it.

"We must be nearing an exit," she said, quickening her pace. But several yards farther, she bumped into a solid wall directly in front of her. Aunt Pitty Pat stumbled against her, and Gaylord flapped his wings to avoid falling on top of them.

"Why are we stopping?" gasped Aunt Pitty Pat as Gaylord helped her back on her feet.

"I'm not sure," said Minabell, trying to keep the worry out of her voice. But there was no doubt about it. The passageway went no farther. "We seem to have come to a dead end," she said finally.

Gaylord disagreed. "There must be an exit nearby, Minabell. I feel a draft on my headcrest."

"I feel the draft, too." Minabell lifted her face, blindly searching the dark. "It's coming from the ceiling." She placed her paws on the wall again and suddenly touched wood. She ran her paw along its surface. It was a wooden step. The first rung in a stepladder built into the wall!

Gaylord gave Minabell a boost up onto the lower rung of the ladder.

She quickly went up the ladder and scrambled through an opening in the ceiling. She found herself in a dimly lit and windy corridor directly above the passageway. Aunt Pitty Pat climbed up next, closely followed by Gaylord.

"Praise the prairie skies!" exclaimed Aunt Pitty Pat. "We can see again."

"We must hurry," Minabell said. "The sun is coming up. Magnus will soon discover we're missing." She hastily led them along the corridor toward the light.

"It's a stairway," her aunt said when they drew near. "Oh, dearie me! I don't know where we are. I'm all turned around. And in my own house, too."

The light and the cold wind were coming from a narrow window on the first landing. They ran up the steps and peeked out. Aunt Pitty Pat shook her head. "I do declare! We're standing right over the manor's front entrance."

The sun was just rising above Indian Mound Hill. It colored the horizon a pale orange and faintly lit the park surrounding the manor.

Directly below them was the statue of Geronimouse. How sad, thought Minabell, to see the great leader holding the skull and crossbones on high.

Minabell longed to climb the flagpole and tear down that ugly rag. How she yearned to replace it with the glorious flag of the sovereign state of Illinois! But this wasn't the time for dreams of valor, she reminded herself. She turned away and followed her companions up the second flight of stairs.

The higher they climbed, the more worried Minabell became. Upward, she thought, was not the way to go if they wanted to escape from the manor. But since this appeared to be the only direction they could go at the moment, she said nothing.

The stairwell grew narrower and the steps

steeper. On the ninth landing, Aunt Pitty Pat slumped to the floor. "Go on up," she said breathlessly. "I'll follow you."

Minabell looked at the square of light above. "Just one more flight," she pleaded. "I think we've come to the top."

"Listen!" said Aunt Pitty Pat. "What's that?"

"It sounds like a bell," Gaylord said.

Whiskers aquiver, Aunt Pitty Pat struggled to her feet, forgetting how tired she was. "Indeed it is a bell, Gaylord. I think we've climbed to Mousehaven Manor's belfry tower. Imagine that! I didn't know there was a way to get up here."

They quickly climbed the last flight and stepped out onto a windswept turret, open on all sides to the sky. In the center of the turret, a great bell hung down from the rafters. Its clapper, lashed by the wind, gave out an occasional metallic clang. A heavy rope was attached to the bell and hung down to the floor. The end of the rope disappeared down a small opening in the floorboards.

"I wonder where the rope goes?" Minabell said.

Aunt Pitty Pat examined it carefully. "This is the bellpull. It runs all the way down to a small room on the first floor. It's used to ring the bell. And it takes two strong rodents, pulling together, to ring it."

As if in answer, the rope twitched and moved downward through the hole. The bell swung slowly at first. Then it picked up speed, its clapper striking with deafening force. Peal after peal resounded in the belfry tower and out over the countryside.

Minabell and her aunt staggered back against the parapet, paws pressed to their ears. With a startled squawk, Gaylord fell backward into the stairwell.

At last the rope stopped moving, and the bell was stilled. Minabell and her aunt took their paws from their ears and stared at the bell in stunned relief.

In the dead silence that followed, they heard a high-pitched, squeaky voice. "Oh, my! What a great ruckus." A second later

Gaylord reappeared in the doorway, none the worse for his fall.

Minabell looked uncertainly at the big bird. "Did you say something, Gaylord?"

"Not I," said the cardinal. He cocked his head, listening. Then he peered up at the rafters above the bell.

There was a soft rustling and a faint murmuring overhead.

"Move over," squeaked the voice.

Another small voice piped up. "Be careful, Percy. You're standing on my head. Please hang still and don't move about so. You're waking everybody up."

"Oh, botheration! Who can sleep in this noisy belfry, anyway?" It was the first little voice again.

The three below could just make out a mass of small, brown-furred creatures clinging to a corner rafter. There was a sudden upheaval in the center of the group.

Someone emerged and, with much muttering and sighing, crawled over the backs of its fellows to a nearby crossbeam. Hanging upside down, the creature moved slowly across the rafter into the light. He blinked his eyes and peered down at them.

"Oh, I say! We have company. How perfectly swell," piped a pleasant little voice. Still hanging head down, the creature unfolded naked, leathery wings. He yawned widely, revealing a full set of fangs set in a tiny blood-red mouth.

"AWWWK!" screeched Gaylord. "It's a vampire bat!"

He flew to the parapet and balanced dangerously close to the edge, ready to take flight. "Minabell, Aunt Pitty Pat! Run for your lives!"

Staring up at the creature, Minabell and her aunt clung to each other, unable to move.

123

17.
Escape

"Oh, I say, my dear fellow!" squeaked the little brown bat. "A vampire bat? Oh, dear me, no! Not a bit of truth in that."

The bat stretched his wings and settled himself more comfortably on his perch. "I rather like to think of myself as a flying rodent." He paused in reflection. "Yes, definitely. That's the way I picture myself — as a flying mouse." He smiled down at Minabell, revealing his fangs again. "Don't you agree, miss?" he inquired shyly.

He did not wait for a reply, but continued, "Ugly creatures, vampire bats. Very unsavory branch of the family." His voice grew faint. "Gives — us — all — a — bad — name -- and . . . " He dozed off in midsentence, emitting a loud, very un-mouselike snore.

"He's fallen asleep," whispered Minabell.

"No, no, little miss," murmured the bat, jerking awake. "I am still among the conscious." He shook himself and swung up to a sitting position on the rafter, folding and unfolding his wings.

Gaylord let out another startled squawk as the upright bat gazed down at them from hooded eyes, set in a small, wrinkled face.

"I do believe introductions are in order," squeaked the bat, politely disregarding Gaylord. "Percival M. Bat, here." He placed a wingtip over his unsightly little mouth and giggled pleasantly. "Do call me Percy," he tittered. "Everybody does."

"Who's everybody?" muttered Gaylord. Percy gestured at the furry group asleep in the alcove. "My family," he said simply.

"There were one hundred and ten of us at last fall's pre-hibernation count."

Gaylord opened his beak to make a rude remark, but Aunt Pitty Pat hastily intervened. "Bats in my belfry. I do declare! You're all most welcome, I'm sure."

Aunt Pitty Pat introduced herself and her companions. She told Percy of the seizure of Mousehaven Manor by the Prairie Pirates, and of their capture and present plight.

"Oh, I say! How dreadful for you." Percy waved a wingtip in the direction of his family. "We all suspected that something must be wrong in the manor. First there was the bell ringing at dawn. Then there was the loud merrymaking at all hours of the night. Hibernating has not been easy, I can tell you." His little mouth gaped in an ear-popping yawn. "What brutes these Prairie Pirates are, I must say."

"They certainly are!" agreed Gaylord. He lowered his headcrest and gave the bat a nod of approval.

Minabell was standing with her back to the parapet, lost in thought. A plan was taking shape in her mind.

The first part of the plan was, of course, to escape from the manor. Once they were free, she could begin the second part of the plan. But first they had to escape. "Yes," she said. "It just might work."

"What might work, mouseling?" asked her aunt. "A prairie pebble for your thoughts."

"Oh, Aunt Pitty Pat, I hope my thoughts will prove to be worth more than a pebble." Minabell looked up at the bat. "Percy, how often do the pirates ring the bell?"

"They ring it once a day — every morning at dawn, little miss. Roll call, I believe they call it."

Gaylord, who was still standing on the top of the parapet, glanced down at the park. "Look, Minabell. They're taking roll call now."

Minabell peeked over the ledge. The Prairie Pirates had assembled directly below, in front of the manor. They stood at attention in two long rows, ready for inspection. From that height she couldn't identify any of her former captors — not even the unpleasant Number Two.

A large rat ambled out of the front entrance. It was Magnus, recognizable even from a distance. Paws on hips, he stood in the snow receiving the hoarsely shouted greetings of his troops: "SUNGAM! SUN-GAA-AM!"

Minabell shuddered and ducked below the parapet. When she dared to peek again, the pirates were marching in review in front of Magnus. Each one, as he passed the leader, called out his number and presented his weapon in a ragged salute.

With a final shout, the troops broke ranks. Some trotted across the park to their guard posts; the rest followed Magnus back inside the manor.

Minabell had seen enough. Their escape was about to be discovered, of this she was certain. And then the pirates would be searching the countryside for them. The time had come for action. She turned to her companions and quickly explained phase one of her plan.

Gaylord and Aunt Pitty Pat gave their wholehearted support. Percy immediately offered his services.

"I'm not at my best flying in sunlight," he apologized. "But I shall welcome the challenge, little miss." So saying, he flapped down from the rafters, and Minabell climbed up on his back.

Aunt Pitty Pat gazed heavenward in silent prayer and climbed aboard Gaylord.

The cardinal, headcrest at the alert, snapped to attention. "Ready for lift-off, Ms. Minabell."

"To Indian Mound Hill," cried Minabell. Clinging tightly to Percy's back-fur, she closed her eyes and dug in her heels. Moments later they were airborne.

Percy dived and swooped in a movement that was very unsettling. But before Minabell had a chance to become airsick, they had landed on Indian Mound Hill. Gaylord and Aunt Pitty Pat were waiting for them under an elm tree.

The cardinal was pacing back and forth in the snow, obviously worried. "The secret agent and the others should be here," he said. "I'm certain this was to be our meeting place. Don't you remember my mentioning this to you in the dungeon, Minabell?"

Minabell did remember. "But don't forget, Gaylord, you were supposed to meet them here last night. When you didn't return, they must have taken cover. They couldn't stay out in the open very long. They would have been spotted by a pirate scouting party." She looked about nervously. "We must find a place to hide, too."

She glanced at the many rocks and boulders strewn over the hilltop. Which one was her rock, the one with her secret cave hidden under it?

She closed her eyes and repeated the Remembering Rhyme. Then she looked about again. The large rock on the far side of the hill, that was the one, she decided.

"Come," Minabell said and quickly led them to the gray boulder. But as they drew near, she became doubtful. Was this the rock? Where was the entryway — the crevice that she had slipped through so easily the day before? Then she realized the entrance was now cleverly concealed. An oblong stone had been fitted into the narrow opening. Chipped and hewn and carefully placed, it appeared to be part of the boulder itself.

Minabell examined the stone. The fine craftwork was unmistakable. "Teena," she whispered. This had to be the work of Teena Chipmunk. No one else in the state did such expert pawwork.

She put her mouth to a crack. "Teena," she called softly. "It's Minabell. Are you in there?"

They strained their ears. But there was only the sound of the wind, and the creaking of the barren branches of the elm tree.

Then there came a low murmur of voices from within. A moment later the stone swung back, and Secret Agent Wendell Weasel stood in the entrance. He looked down at them and released a deep sigh of relief. "Minabell Mouse! Gaylord! And this must be Aunt Pitty Pat. Come in! Come in! We've been waiting for you." He stepped aside, and they entered the dark interior.

When the stone had closed behind them a lamp was lit, revealing the large, warm cave Minabell had so reluctantly left the night before. And there were her friends from Rodentville — Teena Chipmunk, Mumbles Mudhouse Mole, and Gaylord's wife, Olivia Cardinal.

Gaylord rushed into his wife's out-stretched wings. "My dear, Olivia, I have returned!"

18.
The Battle Plan

There was much hugging and laughing, and catching up to do.

Finally when everyone settled down, Minabell and her aunt told of their imprisonment by the Prairie Pirates.

Aunt Pitty Pat assured everybody that she had never been ill and, indeed, had not felt better in mouseyears. "And as for Magnus Rat," she said, drawing herself up to her full height. "Marry that rodent? The very idea!"

Gaylord, eyes flashing, told of his heroic encounter with the pirates. Thrashing his wings, he gave a blow-by-blow account.

"Gaylord, my beloved, remember your heart condition," pleaded Mrs. Cardinal.

But Gaylord's story wasn't finished. "Through the depths of the earth," he cried, "I led us through secret passageways up to the very top of the belfry tower — to FREE-DOM!"

"Baloney," said a low voice, sounding suspiciously like Mumbles. But it was drowned out by the generous congratulations of the others.

A nervous giggle from the back reminded Minabell that she had neglected her mouse-manners. In all the excitement she had forgotten Percy. The shy little bat was introduced, and Minabell told them of his part in their escape.

Minabell clapped her paws for their attention. "I'm afraid the danger isn't over yet. As long as Magnus and his pirates remain on the prairie, none of us will be safe." She placed an arm around her aunt's shoulders. "I think I have a plan that will chase them from our land and return Mousehaven Manor to its rightful owner, Ms. Pitty Pat Mouse."

She looked around at her friends, their faces aglow in the lamplight. "If my plan is to work," she said quietly, "I will need your help."

"Tell us what we can do, Minabell," Teena said.

"You can count on us," mumbled the mole.

"We are yours to command!" cried Gaylord.

"Indeed we are, my dear," murmured his wife.

The secret agent stepped forward. "So, Ms. Minabell Mouse," he said with a twinkle in his eye. "I see you did not take my advice about returning to Rodentville. You were very lucky. It might have gone badly for you. But you are safe now, and that is the important thing. I, too," he added seriously, "would like to help in the recapture of Mousehaven Manor. But first I have a few words I'd like to say to all of you."

The agent paused, his white-furred brow creased in thought. "I have decided," he said finally, "to take you into my confidence."

They were all silent, and the agent continued. "I have had Magnus Rat and his Prairie Pirates under observation for some time. As you know, there are fifty Prairie Pirates. But what you don't know is that each of these pirates is in charge of one of Chicago's fifty city wards. Each pirate commands thousands of rats in his own ward. And Magnus commands the pirates. One word from him and all those rats, from all fifty wards, would come pouring out of Chicago and take over the state of Illinois. We cannot let that happen. As Minabell said, the time has come to take a stand and chase the Prairie Pirates back where they came from before it is too late."

The agent turned to Minabell and addressed her formally. "Ms. Mouse, I would like to hear more about your idea to rid the prairie of this menace. If it should prove to be successful, you will have the heartfelt appreciation of your state and of the ISSP. And I, Secret Agent Wendell Weasel, stand ready to help."

After everybody had eaten a meal of acornburgers provided by Olivia Cardinal, they gathered around Minabell again, as she outlined phase two of her plan. She had left nothing to chance. The idea appeared to be foolproof.

"This is actually a battle plan," said the agent. "And a very good one, too. I can find nothing that needs to be changed."

They worked out an exact timetable, and everyone rehearsed his part in it. The action would start the next morning at dawn. Their signal would be the ringing of the great bell in the belfry tower. After a final discussion and rehearsal, Percy Bat left the hill and flew back to the tower to alert his family.

At midday, the secret agent, who had been standing guard outside the cave, quietly slipped back inside. He held up his paw in silent warning; he had just seen a pirate search party climbing the west side of the hill.

The friends hurriedly pushed the entry stone back in place, sealing it with sand, and put out the lamp. Then they all sat down against the back wall of the cave and waited in silence, hardly daring to breathe.

Soon they heard the heavy footsteps and harsh voices of the pirates as they swarmed over the hillside. From the shouted commands, there was no doubt who they were after. Minabell, Aunt Pitty Pat, and Gaylord had been discovered missing.

The pirates searched in every nook and cranny, even poking around the cave entrance. But so cunningly had Teena fitted the entry stone that the rats passed it by.

Shouts came from overhead as the pirates scrambled up one side of the boulder and down the other, never suspecting what they were hunting was directly underfoot.

Soon there was quiet once again on Indian Mound Hill, and the secret agent gave the all clear signal.

Now it was even more urgent that they get to work on their final preparations. Teena Chipmunk made bows and arrows from the smaller elm branches found under the snow.

But she was afraid the weapons might have to be abandoned for want of proper arrowheads.

Then Minabell remembered her find of two nights ago. She rummaged through her backpack and triumphantly produced the finely crafted arrowhead she had stumbled over on leaving Rodent Run.

But more than one arrowhead was needed. Aunt Pitty Pat reminded everyone they were standing on a historic Illinois Indian site. Perhaps they were standing on an entire store of weapons. And, indeed, this turned out to be the case.

Mumbles Mole dug into the sand floor of the cave and found all the arrowheads they needed, in good condition, ready for use.

At midnight the secret agent slipped past the entry stone and crept down the hill to scout the enemy. He returned at 0200 hours with word that the Prairie Pirates were asleep in the manor. There were only a few hours left until sunup and D-hour at 0600.

19.
Geronimouse!

As the sun crept over the ridge of Indian Mound Hill, the small band of comrades crept down Mousedale's main street. Minabell led the way, carrying her state flag. Close behind walked Teena and Aunt Pitty Pat. Next came Gaylord and Olivia Cardinal, holding Minabell's sleeping bag filled with rocks.

Mumbles brought up the rear with the bows and arrows strapped to his back. He shuffled along, nearsightedly peering into the dark. "This ain't gonna work, I tell ya," he mumbled. "I say we attack them varmints while they're still sleeping."

"Quiet, Mumbles," whispered Minabell. She stopped and silently held up her paw.

They had come to the end of the street. Ahead of them loomed the statue of Geronimouse in the deserted parkway. Beyond stood the manor, dark and forbidding in the pre-dawn gloom.

Minabell gave a low whistle. An answering whistle came from the alley on their left. A moment later Secret Agent Weasel stepped out of the shadows and joined them.

"It's almost time," he said quietly. "It will be daylight soon." He nodded toward the manor. "Luck is with us. The guard has fallen asleep."

Minabell looked across the park. The flares on either side of the manor entrance had gone out. She could just make out the dark shape of the guard sleeping under the portico.

"Perhaps the mole is right," Gaylord whispered. "Maybe we should attack now while they're all asleep and least expect it."

The secret agent frowned. "We will carry out Minabell's plan as we agreed earlier. Is that understood?" He looked slowly around the group. There was no other opposition. "Very well, then," the agent said. "You all know what to do. Take your battle stations, and wait for my command."

❧

The day dawned bleak and cold. Minabell, the secret agent, and the cardinals hid behind the base of Geronimouse. They peeked out anxiously in the half light and watched Aunt Pitty Pat and Mumbles creep past the sleeping guard.

Aunt Pitty Pat's part in the plan was vital. She was the only one who knew the interior of the manor well enough to find her way around it in the dark. With Mumbles' help, she had to get inside the mansion and hide near the front entrance.

When the tower bell rang, the pirates would wake up and assemble outside for roll call as they did every morning. After they were all outside, Aunt Pitty Pat would run to the front door and bolt it, sealing off the rats' retreat back into the manor.

Minabell held her breath as her aunt and the mole tiptoed past the snoring guard. If he should wake up now all their carefully laid plans would come to nothing.

The secret agent leaned forward, one paw on his knife. "Be prepared to run at my command," he whispered. "I'll hold off the guard."

Aunt Pitty Pat and Mumbles hesitated as the pirate, muttering in his sleep, turned over on his side. But his continued snores reassured them. They sprinted for the safety of the manor wall and disappeared around the corner of the building.

Five minutes later Mumbles crept back behind the statue and reported Aunt Pitty

Pat's successful entry into the manor. "We found a kitchen window open, and I boosted her up. And a brave little mouse she is, too," he added.

He was interrupted by the tolling of the bell. Minabell, Teena, and Mumbles snatched up their bows and arrows. Gaylord and his wife stood at attention next to the sleeping bag filled with rocks.

As the last peal of the bell died out, the guard stood up and rubbed the sleep from his eyes. He looked up at the sky and then out over the park. Apparently satisfied, he shuffled over to the entrance and picked up his club.

The door opened, and several sleepy pirates wandered out. They were soon followed by others who straggled out, one by one. They formed two ragged lines facing the door, their backs to the statue.

"I've counted forty-nine," Minabell whispered to the agent. "They're all out except Magnus."

The front door banged open again, and

Magnus Rat appeared. He yawned and scratched his belly. Then he moved out of the shelter of the door, and it slammed shut behind him.

Minabell and Secret Agent Weasel leaped to the top of the statue's pedestal.

"GERONIMOUSE!" cried Minabell, waving her bow in the air. Then she jumped back down to safety behind the pedestal.

As one, the fifty startled pirates turned and stared at the statue.

"Wh — whaz that?" muttered Magnus, peering up bleary-eyed at Geronimouse.

"Magnus Rat," yelled Wendell Weasel, "I arrest you and the Prairie Pirates in the name of the state of Illinois. You have a right to remain silent. Anything you say may be used against you in a court of law."

Magnus shook the sleep from his eyes and came alive. "GET THAT WEASEL!" he bellowed. "PULL THAT SKINNY RODENT DOWN FROM THERE!"

Before the line of rats could move, Wendell shouted a command. "Archers forward!"

Minabell, Teena, and Mumbles stepped from behind the statue, their bows at the ready.

"FIRE!" shouted the agent. Minabell loosed her arrow. It sailed over the pirates and joined the other two arrows in the door behind Magnus, just above his head.

Magnus grabbed at the door latch and tried to escape back into the manor. There was the sound of a heavy door bar being slammed into place from within. Aunt Pitty Pat had bolted the door.

Snarling, Magnus shook the useless latch. Then he wheeled around and shrieked a command to his pirates. "ATTACK — you sniveling cowards!"

Minabell saw Number Two pick up his club. "Charge!" he yelled. The line of rats moved toward them.

The secret agent turned to Gaylord and his wife. "Bombardiers aloft!" he shouted. The cardinals were ready. They snatched up the sleeping bag in their claws and leaped into the air.

"Bombs away!" came the command, and they overturned the sleeping bag, releasing all their ammunition over enemy lines.

Pirates screamed as they were hit and fell to the ground. "Help! Look out! It's raining rocks!" they shouted and turned back toward the manor.

Magnus howled with fury. He ran out from the portico, twirling his war club over his head. "I'll kill the first rat who retreats," he bawled. His club whistled through the air as he raced back and forth behind the lines.

His troops cowered away from him and turned again to their attackers.

Magnus, saliva drooling from his mouth, took the lead. He reached the base of the statue and started to climb up. The secret agent kicked him back down.

The agent looked up at the belfry tower and shouted one last command before he was pulled off the pedestal. "Dive bombers attack!" he yelled. Then he disappeared into the army of rats.

A high-pitched wail came from the belfry tower. All eyes looked up as a V formation of bats, one hundred and ten strong, dived on the enemy. From one hundred and ten little blood-red mouths came a shrieking battle cry. It split the chill December air and numbed the hearts of those below.

Magnus, clutching Wendell Weasel by the throat, gave a quick glance up at the tower. His mouth went slack. With a frightened squeal, he let go of the agent. "VAMPIRE BATS!" he screamed. He dropped his weapon, turned tail, and ran.

The cry was taken up by the other rats. "Vampire bats!" Wild-eyed, they scrambled over each other in a frenzy to get away.

The entire army of Prairie Pirates caught up with Magnus Rat just as he disappeared over the ridge of Indian Mound Hill. They were pursued by one hundred and ten small bats and two large cardinals.

Minabell surveyed the weapon-strewn

battlefield and saw her comrades resting under the portico.

The secret agent was wounded. His ear, badly torn, was being bandaged by Aunt Pitty Pat. When she had finished, he flipped on his walkie-talkie and reported their victory to his superior.

"Much of the credit, sir, should go to Ms. Minabell Mouse and her friends. I am recommending them for citations of bravery and good citizenship."

Minabell removed the tissue paper from around her flag. Then she picked her way over rocks and war clubs to the base of the monument.

She climbed onto the pedestal and gazed up at her ancestor. Geronimouse stood four-square and solid, facing a new day on the prairie.

She quickly shinnied up to the top of the flagpole and removed the tattered skull and crossbones. Then she carefully attached her state flag to the pole.

Minabell watched her spotless white flag unfurl in the sunlight and flutter over the head of Geronimouse. The golden eagle of Illinois flew once again at Mousehaven Manor.

20.
The New Year's Eve Party

*I*n the days that followed, Aunt Pitty Pat and Minabell set the manor to rights. They swept away all the debris and polished every room until the old mansion sparkled like a golden prairie pebble.

"I do declare, Minabell," Aunt Pitty Pat said finally, "this place is about ready for company. But first let's give it the white mitten test."

Putting on a pair of fresh white mittens, Aunt Pitty Pat ran her paws over all the furniture and woodwork. Only when her mittens came away clean, without a hint of dust on them, was she satisfied.

"Now we can have a New Year's Eve party," she said happily.

All of Mousedale was invited. Each village mousewife prepared her favorite recipe and brought it to the manor. The banquet tables were soon piled high with every sort of delicious-smelling dish.

The young rodents, eyes popping, stood on tiptoe to peer over the tabletops at the holiday fare provided by their mothers.

There were roast rutabagas stuffed with hickory nut dressing; shimmering green mounds of gooseberry jello; great tureens of steaming-hot sweet clover soup; platters of acornburgers smothered in wild herb gravy; old-fashioned prairie-grass biscuits, still warm from the oven; tall pitchers of spiced pinecone cider; and all manner of pies and puddings, iced pastries, and candied fruits.

Never before had such a spread been seen in Mousedale or, indeed, in the whole of Sangamon County.

The ballroom shook to the dancing feet of the young buck rodents and their bright-eyed partners. Around and around they whirled, tails flying, as they stomped to the rousing beat of the Rodent Rhythm Boys.

And on the balcony of the main staircase the Melody Mouse Quartet was harmonizing, singing the sentimental old ballads so dear to country creatures.

"Come, Minabell," said Aunt Pitty Pat. "It is time for us to have a talk." They left the happy merrymakers and found a quiet spot in an upstairs parlor.

They sipped glasses of dandelion wine and spoke of matters close to Aunt Pitty Pat's heart. When they were finished Minabell had reached a decision, and her aunt's eyes were shining with happy unshed tears.

"Oh, mouseling!" cried Aunt Pitty Pat. "Let's go downstairs and tell our friends."

They found the guests gathered in the

grand ballroom to say good-bye to the secret agent. The bandage on the handsome weasel's ear gave him a rather rakish air as he shook paws all around.

"I must hurry," he said, buckling on his equipment belt. "I am needed in the sewers of Chicago."

Minabell was sorry to see the agent leave. She walked with him to the front entrance, and they stood in companionable silence for a few moments.

"Ms. Minabell, please remember you can always call on the ISSP if you need assistance."

Then, with a warm nod and a smart salute, Secret Agent Wendell Weasel left Mousehaven Manor.

Minabell stood at the door remembering the garbage-strewn entryway she had stepped into one week ago. What a change had taken place in that one week! The oak floor, now cleaned and polished, gleamed in the overhead light.

She glanced up at the crystal chandelier

softly tinkling above her. Percy Bat was clinging comfortably to the bottom of the light.

"Good night, little miss," murmured Percy, and promptly fell asleep and into deep hibernation. Minabell climbed on a chair and gently removed the empty wine glass from his leathery little claw.

Then she hurried into the grand ballroom and stood beside her aunt, who had asked Gaylord to call everyone to attention.

He raised his headcrest and paced back and forth. "Quiet!" he shouted. "Quiet, everyone! Minabell has an important announcement to make."

The mouseguests stopped talking and looked at Minabell. Small rodents, middle-sized rodents, mother and father rodents, and grizzled-furred old grandmas and grandpas waited expectantly for her to speak.

Minabell took her aunt's paw and stepped forward. She looked out over the roomful of friends and gave Aunt Pitty Pat's paw a small squeeze.

"Dear friends," she said, "after much thought, I have decided to stay in Mousedale and live here at Mousehaven Manor with Aunt Pitty Pat. Forever and ever," she added softly.

A hush fell over the ballroom. Then from the back of the room the tiniest mouse piped up, "Hooray for Mousehaven Manor!"

"Hooray for Minabell and Aunt Pitty Pat!" cried the grown-ups.

"We'll miss you, Minabell," said Teena Chipmunk. Mumbles and the cardinals nodded in silent agreement.

"We will come back to Rodentville often to visit," Minabell assured them.

"You all must come and stay with us here at Mousehaven Manor," said Aunt Pitty Pat. "Every New Year's Eve we'll have a grand party."

Everybody applauded.

Suddenly someone started singing a familiar old ballad and, one by one, the others joined in.

"On this vast prairie,
Oh, spacious land.
On this broad plain
We take our stand.

Oh, Mousehaven Manor,
May you ever be free!
Oh, Mousehaven Manor,
We'll always love thee!"

Minabell put an arm around her aunt and held her close. "Happy New Year, Aunt Pitty Pat!" she whispered.

❧